CALICO ILLUSTRATED CLASSICS

Kenneth Grahame's

The Wind in the Willows

ADAPTED BY: Lisa Mullarkey
ILLUSTRATED BY: Shawna J.C. Tenney

magic wagon

visit us at www.abdopublishing.com

Published by Magic Wagon, a division of the ABDO Group, 8000 West 78th Street, Edina, Minnesota 55439. Copyright © 2010 by Abdo Consulting Group, Inc. International copyrights reserved in all countries. All rights reserved. No part of this book may be reproduced in any form without written permission from the publisher.

Calico Chapter Books™ is a trademark and logo of Magic Wagon.

Printed in the United States of America, Melrose Park, Illinois.
102009
012010

Original text by Kenneth Grahame
Adapted by Lisa Mullarkey
Illustrated by Shawna J.C. Tenney
Edited by Stephanie Hedlund and Rochelle Baltzer
Cover and interior design by Abbey Fitzgerald

F-Jr
MUL

Library of Congress Cataloging-in-Publication Data

Mullarkey, Lisa.
   The wind in the willows / adapted by Lisa Mullarkey ; illustrated by Shawna J.C. Tenney ; based on the works of Kenneth Grahame.
       p. cm. -- (Calico illustrated classics)
   ISBN 978-1-60270-713-9
   [1. Animals--Fiction.] I. Tenney, Shawna, ill. II. Grahame, Kenneth, 1859-1932. Wind in the willows. III. Title.
   PZ7.M91148Wi 2010
   [Fic]--dc22

                                        2009033967

112p.: ill.; 20 cm. Edina, MN: Edina, MN: Magic Wagon, 2010.

Table of Contents

CHAPTER 1

The River Bank

Mole had been working hard all morning long. He was spring cleaning with brooms, dusters, and a pail of whitewash. His eyes were filled with dust. His throat was filled with dust. Splashes of whitewash covered his fur. His back ached.

"I've had enough," said Mole. He bolted out the door without putting on his coat. Something above was calling him up to the sun and air.

So he scraped and scratched and scratched and scraped with his paws until *pop!* His snout came out into the sunlight. Mole found himself rolling in the warm grass of a large meadow.

This is fun! he thought. *This is better than*

whitewashing. The sunshine felt warm on his fur. Soft breezes touched his brow. The songs of birds reminded him how alone he had been underground. Jumping on all four legs at once, he ran across the meadow. His heart raced.

"Stop!" said an old rabbit. "This is a private road. You must pay six pennies to pass."

But Mole didn't stop. He continued exploring the meadow. The birds, flowers, and breeze made him happy. He noticed all the creatures working around him—working while he played! He took great pleasure realizing that the best part of a holiday is not resting but seeing everyone else working.

He didn't think he could feel any happier than he did in the meadow. But then he came upon a river! He had never seen a river before. He was fascinated by the gurgling sound of the water. The glints, gleams, and sparkles mesmerized him.

As he sat on the grass and looked across the river, a dark hole in the bank caught his eye. He dreamed it would be the perfect home for an animal who longed to live by the river. Just then, something popped out of the hole and winked at Mole. It was a little brown face with whiskers. It had small ears and thick, silky hair. It was a water rat!

The two animals stood and stared at each other cautiously.

"Hello, Mole!" said Rat.

"Hello, Rat!" said Mole.

"Would you like to come over?" asked Rat.

Mole was wondering how he'd reach the other side when he saw Rat unfasten a rope and step into a boat. Mole hadn't noticed the boat before. It was painted blue outside and white inside. It was the perfect size for two small animals. Even though Mole wasn't exactly sure what it was, he stepped into it when it arrived.

"This is a wonderful day," said Mole. "I've never been in a boat before."

Rat shoved off. "What?" cried Rat. "Never been in a boat? What have you been doing?

Believe me, there is nothing as good as messing about in boats all day."

"Look out, Rat!" cried Mole suddenly.

It was too late. The boat struck the bank full tilt. Rat lay on his back at the bottom of the boat. His heels were in the air. Rat picked himself up and laughed.

"It doesn't matter if you even get anywhere in a boat. As long as you are in a boat, it's a wonderful day," said Rat.

Mole wiggled his toes as Rat steered toward a dock.

"Why not spend the day with me?" asked Rat. He scurried off the boat and brought back a lunch basket. He lifted the lid to show Mole the treats inside.

Mole couldn't believe his luck. "I can hardly wait to begin." Soon, Mole was lost in his thoughts. He was thinking about this new world he had entered with his new friend. He felt quite fortunate.

After a half hour, Rat felt it was okay to disturb Mole. "I like your jacket very much."

"I beg your pardon," said Mole. "You must think I've been rude just staring at the river all this time. This is all so new to me." He sucked in his breath. "So this is a river!"

"*The* river," corrected Rat.

"What a jolly life you have," said Mole.

Rat agreed. "It's my world. I don't want any other. Whether it's winter, spring, summer, or fall, the river is always exciting."

"Isn't it dull sometimes?" asked Mole. "Just you and the river?"

Rat laughed. "You *are* new at this. Actually, the bank is crowded with animals. Otters, kingfishers, moorhens, and all sorts of creatures live here. They always want to do something!"

"What lies over there?" asked Mole, waving a paw toward the woods on one side of the river.

"That? Oh, just the Wild Wood," said Rat. "We riverbankers don't go in there too often."

"Why not?" asked Mole nervously. "Aren't there nice animals in there?"

"Well," replied the Rat, "the squirrels are all right. The rabbits are mixed. Some are nice. Others? Well, not so much." Then he smiled. "And of course Badger lives there. He lives in the heart of it. He wouldn't move anywhere else. Nobody would ever bother Badger."

"Who would try?" asked Mole.

"Foxes and weasels and so on," said Rat. "I'm friends with all of them, but you can't really trust them."

Mole knew that he shouldn't dwell on possible trouble ahead, so he changed the subject. "And what's beyond the Wild Wood?"

"Ah," said Rat. "Beyond the Wild Wood is the Wide World. I've never been there and I'll never go there. You won't either if you have any sense at all." The Rat sighed. "Please don't ever refer to it again."

Mole shuddered and promised to never mention the Wide World again.

Meeting New Friends

Mole and Rat continued on their adventure. Rat brought the boat alongside the bank and helped Mole to shore. Rat gave the wicker basket to Mole. Mole wanted to empty the basket himself to thank Rat for lunch.

Mole shook out the tablecloth and lay it down on the grass. Then, he took out all sorts of mysterious packets and lay them out.

Finally Rat said, "Dig in."

Mole was happy to obey the orders.

As they ate, Rat noticed Mole staring at something. "What are you looking at?"

"I see bubbles in the water," said Mole. "A streak of bubbles traveling along the surface. It looks funny."

"Bubbles?" asked Rat. He perked up as a broad, glistening muzzle popped up on the bank. It was Otter. He hauled himself out of the water and shook his coat.

"Greedy!" said Otter. "Why didn't you invite me, Ratty?"

"This is an impromptu affair," said Rat. "But please meet my friend, Mr. Mole."

"Nice to meet you," said Otter. "Such a rumpus everywhere. All the world seems out on the river today. I came here to get a moment's peace and found you two."

Just then, there was a slight rustle behind them. Badger peered out from behind a bush.

"Come out, Badger."

Badger trotted forward a pace or two and then grunted. "Hmpf! Company." He turned his back and disappeared.

"That's the sort of fellow he is," said Rat. "Simply hates society and the world at times. We won't see any more of him today."

Otter then gave everyone the rundown on who was on the river that day. He enjoyed speaking of Toad, who had a new boat.

"Toad often has new boats and grows tired of them easily. It won't be long before he has a new boat and grows bored of that one, too."

It was only minutes later that they spied Toad working hard in his boat to keep it steady. Rat stood and waved him over. Toad shook his head and returned to his work.

"If he doesn't steady that boat, he'll be in the water soon enough," said Rat, laughing.

"Of course he will," said Otter. "Did I ever tell you the time Toad . . ." But he didn't finish. Instead, Otter was off in the water chasing a mayfly. Although they couldn't see Otter in the water, they followed the stream of bubbles on the surface.

Rat hummed a tune and didn't mention Otter's sudden disappearance. Mole didn't want to appear rude, so he didn't mention it either.

"I think we should be moving along," said Rat. "I'll pack up our lunch basket."

"Allow me," said Mole.

Packing up the basket wasn't nearly as much fun as unpacking it. But Mole enjoyed it because he enjoyed everything about river life.

After he had finished, he didn't even mind when Rat laughed about the plate, fork, and mustard bowl that Mole had forgotten to pack away.

The afternoon sun was getting low. Rat gently rowed toward home in a dreamy mood. Mole was feeling content and already at home in the boat. "Please, Rat. May I row the boat?"

Rat shook his head and smiled. "Not yet, my young friend. Wait until you've had a few lessons. It's not as easy as it looks."

Mole was quiet for a few minutes. But then he began to feel a bit jealous of Rat. He started to think that he would indeed be able to row the boat without lessons.

Mole jumped up and seized the oars so suddenly that Rat was taken by surprise and fell backward. For the second time that day, Rat's feet were up in the air. Mole took his place and started rowing with confidence.

"Stop!" yelled Rat. "You'll tip us over."

Mole flung his oars back and made a great dig in the water. He missed the surface altogether and his legs flew up above his head. He suddenly found himself lying on top of Rat!

Shocked, Mole reached for the side of the boat and in the next moment—*sploosh!* Over went the boat. Mole struggled in the water. He felt a paw grip his neck and heard Rat laughing.

It only took Rat a minute to propel Mole safely to shore. "Dry off, Mole, while I get the picnic basket at the bottom of the river." Rat quickly turned the boat right side up and got the basket.

"Ratty, my generous friend," said Mole, "I am sorry for the way I acted. Will you forgive me?"

"What's a little wet to a water rat?" asked Rat cheerily. "I'm in the water more than I'm out of it most days. Why don't you come and stay with me awhile? I'll teach you to row and swim. You'll soon be as good in the water as any of us."

Mole was so touched by Rat's generous offer that he had to wipe away a tear with his paw.

Rat brought Mole home and lit a fire for him. He fetched slippers and a robe for him. Mole was thrilled to listen to the river adventures that Rat spoke of.

Rat told stories deep into the evening until Mole fell asleep. As he drifted off to sleep, Mole thought about how happy he was with his new friend.

This was the first day of their many adventures together. Mole did indeed learn to swim and row. But he learned more than swimming and rowing during those first months together. Mole learned the language of the river and came to understand the whispers of the wind.

CHAPTER 3

Toad Hall

"Ratty," said Mole suddenly one bright summer morning, "if you please, I would like you to take me to meet Mr. Toad."

"Why certainly," said Rat. He jumped up and put his poetry aside. "Get the boat out and we'll paddle up at once. It's never a bad time to call on Mr. Toad. He's always glad to see you and always sad to see you go."

"He must be a nice animal," said Mole as he grabbed the oars.

Rat settled into the stern and took hold of the oars. "He is indeed. So good-natured and so caring. Very affectionate. Perhaps not the most clever. We can't all be geniuses you know."

Rat smiled and started rowing. "He's a bit conceited and boastful. But, a good animal indeed."

Rounding a bend in the river, they came in sight of a handsome, dignified old house with red bricks. The lawns were well kept and reached down to the water's edge.

"There's Toad Hall," said Rat. "And that creek on the left leads to his boathouse. That's where we'll leave the boat. The stables are over there to the right. Straight ahead is the banquet hall. Toad is rather rich, you know. He has the nicest house in these parts." He stepped off the boat. "Of course, I'd never tell that to Toad!"

They headed up the bank and passed the boathouse. Rows of boats were lined up and slung from the crossbeams. Some were hauled up on a slip. None were in the water. It looked as if no one had visited the boathouse in a long time.

Rat said, "Now I understand. Toad's tired of boating. Done with it. I wonder what new fad he's taken up now? I suppose we'll find out soon enough."

They came upon Toad resting in a wicker chair with a large map spread out on his knees.

"Hooray!" Toad cried, jumping up to see them. "This is splendid." He shook both their paws warmly, never waiting for an introduction to Mole. "I was just about to send a boat for you, Ratty. I am so lucky you both turned up now."

"Let's sit a bit, Toady," said Rat, throwing himself down in a chair. Mole sat down beside him and complimented Toad on his fine house.

"Finest house on the whole river," boasted Toad. "Or anywhere else for that matter."

Rat nudged Mole and snickered. Toad saw it and laughed. "You know it's just how I am, Ratty! It's my way to think highly of myself and my home. And you know that you agree it's the finest house here! Anyway, I need you, Ratty."

"To help you row?" asked Rat. "You still splash a great deal. With great patience, care, and some coaching—"

"Boating? Oh, no! No boating!" said Toad. "That's silly boyish stuff. I've given that up long ago. Sheer waste of time. No, I discovered something much better."

Toad led his friends to the stable. There, they saw a caravan. A car on wheels drawn by a horse! It was shiny, new, and painted a canary yellow and green. It had red wheels.

"There you are," said Toad. "This is real life. The open road! The dusty highway! Camps, villages, towns, and cities! Here today and up and off somewhere new tomorrow. Travel! The whole world before you! This is the finest cart of its kind ever built without exception. Come look at the arrangements. Planned them all myself!"

Mole was very excited and interested. He followed Toad eagerly up the steps and into the caravan. Rat snorted. He thrust his hands into his pockets. He didn't budge.

Toad stepped inside and proudly said, "It has everything you could possibly want inside. Look how comfortable it is."

Mole noticed little sleeping bunks and a table that folded up against the wall. There was also a stove, lockers, bookshelves, pots, jugs, and even a birdcage with a bird inside.

"All complete," said Toad as he pulled open a locker. "Look! Biscuits, sardines, lobster, bacon, and jam. Nothing has been forgotten. We'll have everything we'll need this afternoon."

"I beg your pardon, Toad," said Rat. "Did I hear you say *we'll*? 'We'll have everything we need'?"

"You must come, Ratty. Don't start talking in that stiff and snitty way. It will be an adventure. Don't stick to your boat your whole life. You can't live in a hole forever. I want to show you the world. I'm going to make an animal of you, my boy."

"I don't care," said Rat. "I'm not coming and that's that. I love the river, and I'll stick to it. Mole is going to stick with me, too. Aren't you, Mole?"

"Of course I am, Rat," said Mole loyally. "I'll always stick with you, Rat. But it does all sound rather fun."

Poor Mole! His adventures were all so new and thrilling. The thought of going with Toad appealed to him, but he didn't dare let his new friend down.

Rat saw the temptation in Mole's heart. The excitement of a new adventure. He hated disappointing people, and he was so fond of Mole.

By the time lunch was over, Rat decided he could not bear to disappoint his two friends. Soon, all three were making plans for their adventure. In no time, they were off on the dusty road.

CHAPTER 4

The Open Road

Late in the evening, tired and happy and miles from home, the three friends had supper. While they ate, their horse rested and grazed.

Toad talked about all he was planning to do on the open road. As he spoke, the stars grew fuller and larger all around them. A yellow moon appeared to keep them company.

At last, they went to their bunks in the cart. Toad sleepily said, "Well, good night, fellows. This is a real life for a gentleman. Talk about your old river."

Rat was patient. "I don't talk about my river. You know I don't, Toad. But I think about it." Then, in a lower tone, he said, "I think about it all the time."

Mole reached out from under his blanket, felt for Rat's hand, and gave it a squeeze. "If you are unhappy on the road, I'll go back home with you. Maybe we should wake up early? Very early and go back to our dear old hole on the river."

"Thank you, Mole," said Rat. "But I will stick it out. I have to watch after Toady to make sure he's safe. Besides, this is just another fad. He'll tire of it soon enough."

The end was even nearer than Rat had realized.

⚜

The next day, the friends strolled along the road. Mole was by the horse's head talking to him. The horse had complained that he felt left out of conversations. Mole wanted to make it up to him. Toad and Rat were talking to each other. At least Toad was talking. Rat was listening. Behind them, they heard a drone of a distant bee.

Glancing back, they saw a small cloud of dust. The dust was soon coming at them at full speed. They tried to ignore it and resumed their conversation. But an instant later, a blast of wind and a whirl of sound made them jump into the nearest ditch. They hopped out of the way just in time to see a motorcar whirl by them. The driver hugged its wheel and smiled. Soon enough, it droned away from them.

The ruckus scared the old, gray horse, making his cart tumble over into a deep ditch. It wavered a moment before a crash could be heard. The canary-colored cart, Toad's pride and joy, lay in ruins. A total wreck!

Rat shook his hands. "These villains! Scoundrels! Road hogs! I'll have the law on you! I'll report you to the police!" It reminded him of the times boaters drove too near the bank and flooded his parlor carpet at home.

Toad was sitting in the road staring as if he was looking for the disappearing car. Mole was busy trying to quiet the horse.

Rat ran over to the ditch to see the cart. Panels and windows were smashed. Axels were hopelessly bent. One wheel was missing. Sardine tins were scattered about. The bird was in its cage sobbing to be let out.

"Come help us, Toad!"

But Toad stayed there with a silly look on his face. "Glorious sight! The poetry of motion. The *real* way to travel! The *only* way to travel! And to think I thought my cart was good. I was speaking nonsense!"

Rat rolled his eyes. Toad was talking his nonsense again!

"Let's go," said Rat to Mole. "The nearest town is miles away."

"What about Toad?" asked Mole.

"He's moving on to yet another hobby—motorcars!" Just then, Rat turned to Toad. "You need to visit the police station and report that driver. Then, we need to fix the cart."

Toad looked puzzled. "Me? Complain about that beautiful vision? Mend the cart?

I'm done with carts forever. I never want to hear the word again. It's the motorcar I want. It's the motorcar I must have! I long for the dust clouds that will spring up behind me as I speed on my reckless way! What carts I shall fling carelessly into the ditch in the wake of my coming down the open road!"

Rat looked at Mole. "He's hopeless! Next time he wants to go adventuring again, I shall decline!"

Mole and Rat made it to the town with Toad still blabbering. It wasn't long before they left the horse at an inn stable and found a boat. They rowed home. To their *real* home on the river.

The following evening, Mole went fishing. Rat came by to find him. "Have you heard? It's all the news along the bank," said Rat. "Everybody's talking about it. Toad went up to town by train this morning. He ordered a large and very expensive motorcar."

The Wild Wood

Mole had long wanted to meet Badger. By all accounts, he seemed like an important person. One day Mole asked, "Couldn't you ask him over for dinner?"

"He wouldn't come," said Rat. "Badger hates invitations of any sort. He hates society, dinners, and that sort of thing."

"Why don't we go and see him?" asked Mole.

"Oh, he wouldn't like that at all," said Rat. "He's so shy, he'd be offended. I've never called on him in his own home myself. He simply would not like it. Not one bit. Besides, it's quite out of the question because he lives in the middle of the Wild Wood."

"You told me the Wild Wood was all right."

"Well it is," said Rat. "But I don't think he'd be there this time of year anyway. We'll just wait for him to drop by. If you wait patiently, he will show up sooner or later."

Mole waited but Badger never did stop by for a visit. A whole summer passed and winter brought no sign of him either.

Mole and Rat filled the shorter winter days by telling stories around the fire. Mole often listened to Rat's poetry. Sometimes Rat would nap in his armchair to pass the time. So one day when Rat fell asleep, Mole slipped out and headed toward the Wild Wood. He would find Mr. Badger himself!

When he first entered the Wild Wood, he didn't feel afraid. Twigs crackled under his feet. Logs tripped him. It was fun and exciting. But soon, light faded as he went farther into the Wild Wood. Everything became still.

Suddenly, he thought he saw faces everywhere he looked. They were looking out from holes and tree stumps. He walked faster telling himself not to imagine things.

Then the whistling began. At first, it seemed far behind him. But now it seemed that it was ahead of him. He hesitated and wanted to turn back. But he was too afraid to go back. Too afraid to walk forward.

Then the pattering began. He thought it was falling leaves at first. But the sound grew louder. Suddenly, a rabbit dashed past, his eyes staring. "Get out now, you fool." It disappeared into a hole.

In a panic, Mole started to run. He finally found a deep hollow of an old beech tree. Would he be safe there? He had no choice but to hide inside.

He lay there and trembled as he listened to the whistling and patterings in the Wild Wood. It was his darkest moment. The moment Rat had tried to warn him about: the Terror of the Wild Wood!

Meanwhile, Rat woke up and started working on his poems. When he asked Mole for help, he got no reply.

"Mole! Where are you?" shouted Rat as he searched the house. He noticed that Mole's hat wasn't on the peg. His boots were gone, too! Rat left the house and carefully examined the muddy ground. He easily found Mole's tracks. When he saw that they led straight into the Wild Wood, he knew he must go and rescue Mole!

Rat stood in deep thought for a minute or two before returning to the house. He strapped a belt around his waist, shoved a pistol into it, and quickly set off toward the Wild Wood.

It was getting dark by the time Rat entered the Wild Wood. He hunted through the woods for an hour when he heard a faint cry. "Ratty, is that you?"

Rat crept into the hollow and saw Mole trembling.

"I've been so frightened," said Mole.

"I understand, Mole. But you shouldn't have come here. We riverbankers never come here by ourselves. One must know signals, signs, and passwords. You must know how to trick and dodge in here."

"Surely the brave Mr. Toad wouldn't mind coming here by himself?" sobbed Mole.

Rat laughed. "He'd never come alone, Mole. Never!"

Rat's laughter made Mole feel a bit better. A bit braver.

As they were about to go home, Rat noticed the snow. It looked like a completely different woods!

"It's hard to see where we are," said Rat. "Everything looks so different."

After two hours of travel, they were exhausted. They sat on an old tree trunk to rest. The snow was almost impossible to walk through. They fell into hole after hole and were soaking wet. Rat felt it was best to look for shelter for the evening.

The two friends struggled on. Suddenly, Mole tripped and fell on his face. "Oh, my leg!"

Knowing Mole couldn't travel any farther, Rat started scratching at the ground. "Hooray! Look what I've found!'

Mole hobbled over to see it. "A door scraper?"

Anyone who visited the Wild Wood knew that along with a door scraper comes a door. A few scratches later uncovered a doormat. Then, Rat attacked the snowbank beside them. He dug faster and faster.

In no time, a green door stood beside them. It was a dark green door. An iron bellpull hung by the side. Below it, on a small brass plate, engraved in capital letters, they read MR. BADGER.

Mole fell backward on the snow from sheer surprise. "Rat! You're a wonder! If only I had your brains!"

"Are you going to sit in the snow all night and talk?" asked Rat as he attacked the door with his stick. "Get up at once and ring that bell!"

Mole sprang up at the bellpull. He clutched it and swung as both feet glided off the ground. From quite a far way off, they could faintly hear a deep toned bell respond.

CHAPTER 6

Mr. Badger's Home

After what seemed like a long time, the door opened a few inches. A long snout and sleepy eyes peered out. "Who is it disturbing me at this hour? Speak up!"

"Oh, Badger," cried Rat. "Please let us in. It's me and my friend, Mole. We've lost our way in the snow."

"My dear little man!" exclaimed Badger. "Come in both of you. Well, I never! Lost in the snow! And in the Wild Wood in the night! Do come in."

Since Badger had been on his way to bed when he heard the bell, he stood in the hallway in his dressing gown. He looked kindly at Mole and Rat and patted them on the head.

"This is not the sort of evening for small animals to be out and about." He led them into the kitchen, where they warmed up by the fire.

The kitchen was full of treasures! Rows of spotless plates winked from the shelves of the dresser. Hams and herbs hung from the rafters. There were nets of onions and baskets of eggs. Badger had enough for a feast!

Badger made them take off their wet clothes and gave them dry ones. He fixed them something to eat. While they ate, he tended to Mole's shin and mended it until it was good as new. Sitting by the fire eating and sipping tea, it wasn't long before the cold, damp Wild Wood seemed miles away to Rat and Mole.

They shared stories. Never once did Badger ask them not to talk with their mouths full or comment when they placed their elbows on the table. Since Badger never went outside or fancied a party, he wasn't into animal etiquette.

As he listened to Mole's tale of the Wild Wood, he never once said, "That was silly" or

"You should have listened to Rat." Mole liked him at once.

After they finished their meal, Badger asked, "How's old Toad doing?"

"From bad to worse," said Rat. "Another smashup last week. A bad one. He insists on driving himself, but he simply can't do it. Nobody can teach him anything."

"How many has he had?" asked Badger.

"Smashes or machines?" asked Rat. He sighed. "That would be seven for both!"

Mole added, "He's been in the hospital three times. He's paid a lot of fines."

"That's part of the problem," said Rat. "We all know he's rich, but Toad isn't a millionaire. We are his friends and ought to do something."

But Mole and Rat knew the rules of animal etiquette. No one can do anything strenuous or moderately active during the off-season of winter. They had to rest as much as possible.

"Once winter is over, we'll do something," agreed Badger. "We'll take Toad aside and bring him back to reason. We'll stand for no nonsense. We'll make him a sensible Toad."

After all that talk, the three went to bed. The next morning, when Rat and Mole awoke, breakfast was waiting for them.

Within minutes, Otter appeared at Badger's door. "Thought I'd find you here. Everyone along the riverbank was worried when you didn't arrive home. We were worried something terrible had happened. But I knew that if you were in a fix, you'd go straight to Badger."

"Weren't you nervous coming by yourself through the Wild Wood?" asked Mole.

"Nervous?" Otter showed a gleaming set of teeth as he laughed. "I'm just frightfully hungry."

Mole fried him up a slice of ham while Otter and Rat started talking river talk.

Soon Mole and Badger started to speak. Mole told Badger how cozy and comfortable he felt in his underground home. "Once underground, you know where you are. Nothing can happen to you. Nothing can get at you."

Badger beamed. "Yes! That's exactly how I feel. There's no peace or tranquility except underground. If you want your home to expand, dig and scrape a little and there you are! If you feel your house is too big, stop up a hole or two. No worrying about the weather either."

Mole agreed and the two soon became fast friends for life.

Badger continued, "Look at Rat. A couple of feet of floodwater and he has to move to higher ground. And Toad. Nothing against Toad Hall, it is the best house in these parts, but suppose a fire breaks out? A window breaks? What would Toad do? Up and out of doors is good to roam around in but underground? That's my idea of home."

After lunch, Badger grabbed a lantern and took Mole on a tour of his home. Soon, they were in tunnels, passages, and hallways. Mole couldn't believe how big they were! Mole admired every nook and cranny. Each pillar, arch, and crammed storage chamber delighted him.

"How did you ever find the time to do all of this?" he asked.

Badger answered matter-of-factly, "I didn't do it. I only cleaned out the passages and chambers. Long ago, in the Wild Wood, there was a city of people. Where we're standing, they talked, walked, and slept. Who knows where they went? But we badgers stay forever. When they left, trees sprouted and more animals came. Many helped build these homes. The Wild Wood is now filled with good, bad, and indifferent animals."

"I met some of those bad animals on my way here." Mole sighed.

'They're not so bad, really, Mole. I'll pass the word around that you're a friend of mine. You won't be bothered anymore."

When they returned to the kitchen, Rat was pacing nervously. He felt too confined underground. "It's time we leave, Mole. We don't want to spend another night in the Wild Wood."

"I'll come with you," said Otter. "I know my way through the Wild Wood blindfolded."

"No worries for any of you," said Badger. "My tunnels go farther than you think. I have several bolt-holes that will lead directly to the edge of the wood. I just don't tell too many animals about them."

Rat, Mole, and Otter smiled. Badger was always full of surprises!

Home Sweet Home

Once far away from the Wild Wood, Otter departed from his friends. Rat and Mole continued on their journey home, too. They came upon a village. Since it was a cold, winter night, they knew they'd be safe walking the streets. The people were surely all snug inside sitting around fires. No one would be out and about to bother them.

Mole and Rat looked in each window as they passed. They saw a cat being stroked, a sleepy child being carried off to bed, and a woman reading with a cup of tea. It made Mole miss the coziness of his own home that he had left long ago.

Once beyond the village, they could smell the friendly fields again. They plodded along toward home. Each was lost in his own thoughts. Rat was a bit ahead of Mole.

Suddenly, Mole stopped dead in his tracks. His nose twitched. He smelled something familiar. Something wonderful. A rush of old memories flooded every one of his senses. He took another sniff and knew what the wonderful smell was. *Home!*

Mole looked around. Below him, close by, was the home he had left. He was sure of it! It was a small, poorly furnished home, but the home he was happy to get back to after his day's work.

It occurred to him that the home must have been happy with him, too. It was calling him back now. He continued sniffing the ground as his heart raced.

"Stop, Ratty!" pleaded Mole. "I've come across the most wonderful smell. It's my old home. I must go to it."

Rat was too far ahead to clearly hear what Mole had said. "Mole, we mustn't stop now. Snow is coming again. Let's get moving. Be a good fellow."

Mole sat in the middle of the road and sobbed. Although he wanted to find his home, he felt loyal to Rat. So, he got up and continued to follow him. When he finally caught up to Rat, he couldn't contain his sadness. He burst into tears once more.

Rat was shocked at Mole's grief and sadness. "What's troubling you?"

Mole found it difficult to get the words out. "I know it's shabby. Dingy. Not like your cozy home. Not like Toad's beautiful hall or even Badger's great house. But it was my little home. I was quite fond of it. I went away and forgot all about it. But now . . ." Mole sniffed the air once more. "I smell it. My heart might break if I don't go back. But you wouldn't go back, Rat. You wouldn't turn back."

Rat was shocked. "Oh, dear. Of course, Mole. I didn't hear you. Let's go find that house of yours."

In no time, the delicious, homey smells were coming through once more. Mole's nose quivered in the air. Suddenly, Mole dived down a hole. Rat followed. It was airless and small. The earthy smell was strong.

At the end of the tunnel, the two stood in a tiny space. Mole lit a match. Standing before them was Mole's front door with *Mole End* painted neatly on it above the bellpull.

Mole lit the lantern over the bellpull. In an instant, he could see his wire baskets of ferns! A garden seat stood on one side of the door. His statues and benches lined the wall. Small tabletops were covered with dust. The dust was everywhere! In the courtyard was a pond with goldfish swimming around.

Mole's face beamed at the sight of all these objects so dear to him. He hurried through the door and lit a lamp in the hall. His home looked deserted and forgotten.

"Oh, Ratty! Why did I ever bring you to this mess?" Mole said.

Rat paid no attention. "Mole, this is splendid!" He scurried around inspecting cupboards and lighting lamps and candles. "Everything has a place! I'll fetch some wood while you tidy up a bit."

Mole was delighted his good friend was excited about his house. "I wish I had some food, Ratty. You must be hungry. I don't even have a crumb."

In a flash, Rat was in drawers and cupboards finding scraps of food long forgotten. As they started their meal, the doorbell rang. It was the field mice who came around singing Christmas carols every year. Mole was touched that they remembered him once again this year.

They listened to the mice sing and invited them in to enjoy what scraps they had. As they ate, they talked about old times. The mice gave Mole all the latest gossip.

After many hours, the mice left and Rat went to bed. Mole lingered by the fire. He saw clearly how plain and simple everything was. But he knew how much it meant to him. It was his home. It was where his heart was. But Mole didn't want to abandon his new home with Rat by the river. For the river called to him as well.

Mole knew he must return to the river with Ratty. But in his heart he felt strong knowing that he always had this place to call home and to return to whenever it called for him. He knew he would be leaving tomorrow to carry on with Rat. But he also knew that he could always count on being welcomed back. Always.

Mr. Toad

It was bright and early one summer morning when a heavy knock came to the door. Mole flung the door open. "Badger! So good to see you!"

It was a wonderful thing indeed that Badger paid them a visit. It was not something he often did.

Badger looked serious. "The hour has come."

"What hour?" asked Rat as he glanced at the clock on the mantle.

"Why Toad's hour! I told you I would speak to him when the time was right. That time has arrived," Badger answered.

Mole cheered. "Hooray! We'll teach him to be a sensible Toad!"

"This very morning," said Badger, "another new motorcar will arrive at Toad Hall. So we must turn him into a sensible Toad today."

They walked in single file toward Toad Hall. When they arrived, a shiny red motorcar was in front of the house. Mr. Toad was standing nearby in goggles, gloves, and a large overcoat.

"Hello, fellows!" Toad cried. "You are just in time to come with me on a jolly ride!" He heart drooped as he noticed the serious look on his friends' faces.

Mole and Rat hustled Toad inside. Badger explained to the chauffeur that his services wouldn't be needed. "Mr. Toad has changed his mind. He no longer wants this car." Then he followed the others inside.

"Now then," Badger said to Toad. "Take off those ridiculous gloves and goggles."

Toad was outraged. "I demand an explanation."

"You knew it must come to this, Toad," said Badger. "You've spent all the money your father left you. Your driving is bad. You've had too many crashes and smashes. We animals will not allow you to make a fool out of yourself any longer."

Badger took Toad firmly by the arm and led him into the parlor. "We're going to have a talk, Toad. You will become a sensible Toad today." He closed the door behind him leaving Rat and Mole behind.

"What good will talking do?" asked Rat. "Talking won't cure him. He'll say anything Badger wants him to say."

Rat and Mole settled into armchairs and waited patiently. At times, they could hear Badger's voice rise followed by sobs from Toad. Finally, after an hour, the door opened. Toad walked slowly out with his head down and shoulders slumped.

"My friends," said Badger, "I am pleased to inform you that Toad has seen the error of his ways. He is sorry for his reckless behavior."

"That's very good news," said Mole.

Rat wasn't so sure. He spotted a gleam in Toad's eyes.

"Toad," said Badger, "repeat how sorry you are."

There was a long pause. Then Toad stomped his foot. "No! I am not sorry. Driving a motorcar is a glorious experience!"

Badger looked shocked. "Didn't you apologize and admit the error of your ways in there?"

"I would have said anything," laughed Toad. "The only promise I will keep is this one. I promise to get into the very first motorcar I see."

"Very well then," said Badger as he stood. "You have often asked us to come live with you at Toad Hall. Today, we accept your invitation. We will take care of you until you come to your senses. Think of the fun we'll have together!"

The friends carried Toad up the stairs kicking and screaming. "It's for your own good," they said.

Each night, the animals took turns sleeping in Toad's room. They watched as he turned his furniture into motorcars and pretended to drive around. They watched him get angry and then depressed. They hoped that he would eventually agree with them.

One fine morning, Rat went upstairs to see Toad. "The others are out. What would you like to do today?"

"I'm not feeling well, Rat. I'm afraid I need a doctor at once. I couldn't jump out of bed if I tried," he said in a weak voice.

Rat didn't think Toad looked too sick. But the more he spoke to Toad, the more concerned he became.

"I'm afraid my time is coming to an end," said Toad.

"Oh, my," said Rat. "You must be ill!" At once, Rat ran out the door to fetch a doctor.

As soon as Rat left, Toad hopped out of bed and peered out the window. Once Rat disappeared, he grabbed money out of his drawer. Then, he quickly knotted his sheets together and scrambled out the window to the ground below. Toad felt clever and important!

When Rat returned, he learned of Toad's escape. "He tricked you," said Mole.

"He did indeed," said Badger looking annoyed. "But we'll stay here until Toad returns. He'll be back by stretcher or the police at any time I'm sure."

Meanwhile, it didn't take too long before Toad heard the sound of a motorcar coming down the street. He watched from afar and trembled as he looked at it.

When the owners went inside an inn for a bite to eat, Toad went closer to admire the car. What harm could there be just looking at it?

Toad walked around the car inspecting it. *I wonder if this sort of car starts easily,* he thought.

Without knowing what he was doing, he found himself at the steering wheel and driving the car! Soon Toad was in the open country.

He felt wonderful! Nothing could stop him now!

That was his last thought before he woke up in a dungeon with an officer standing guard. "You have stolen a motorcar. You are a bad driver. You insulted the officers. You are sentenced to twenty years in jail."

The guard put his hand on the miserable Toad's shoulder. The rusty key creaked in the lock. The great door clanged behind him. Toad was now a prisoner in the most remote dungeon in one of the strongest castles around.

What will become of me? wondered Toad. *If only I had listened to my friends. If only they had made me a sensible Toad.*

Toad's Adventures

Toad passed the days and nights for several weeks by refusing meals. Each time the guard brought food to him, he sent it away. Finally, the guard stopped going to Toad's cell altogether.

The guard, however, had a kindhearted daughter. She was particularly fond of animals. One day, the daughter said, "Father! I can't bear to see that poor beast so unhappy. He's getting too thin. Can I please take care of him? I'll feed him from my hand."

The man was tired of Toad and agreed to let his daughter do as she pleased. So that day, she knocked on the door of Toad's cell.

"Now cheer up, Toad. Sit up and dry your

eyes. Be a sensible animal. Do try to eat a bit of this dinner. I've brought you mine hot from the oven."

Toad couldn't be persuaded that easily. He kicked and screamed and refused to be comforted. The girl had no choice but to leave. As she left, she pushed the plate toward him.

Alone, he couldn't help but smell the cabbage. The more he sniffed, the hungrier he was. The more he ate, the happier he became. His mind started to think of poetry, meadows, kitchen gardens, and the comforting clink of dishes at Toad Hall. He thought of his friends.

He was feeling much better by the time the girl returned hours later. This time, she brought a cup of tea as well as a plate of toast. Toad sat up and dried his eyes. He sipped his tea and munched his toast. Soon, he was sharing his life story with the girl.

"Tell me about Toad Hall," she said. And he did. He described the boathouse, the fish pond, the stables, and the henhouse. He then told her about the fun he had had with his friends as they sat telling stories and singing songs.

Toad and the girl had many interesting talks together. As the days passed, she grew even more fond of Toad. She knew it was a great shame that the poor animal should be locked up for such a small crime. Toad, of course, in all his vanity, thought that perhaps she loved him. He was, after all, the grand Mr. Toad!

One morning, as Toad talked, the girl hushed him. "Toad, please listen. I have an aunt who is a washerwoman. She washes all the clothes for the prisoners in this castle. She takes it out to wash on Monday morning and returns it Friday evening. Today is Thursday. She'll be back tomorrow."

She leaned in close. "You are very rich from what you say. She's poor. I think you two could come to an agreement. If you pay her a few coins, she will give you her clothes. Then, you could dress in them and escape this castle. Every guard would think you were her."

Toad crossed his arms. "You certainly wouldn't have Mr. Toad of Toad Hall, going about the county dressed as a washerwoman!"

"Then I suppose you shall be in here for twenty years!" replied the girl.

Toad knew he had sounded ungrateful. "You are a good, kind girl. I am indeed a proud and silly Toad. Introduce me to your worthy aunt."

The next evening, the girl ushered her aunt into Toad's cell. The woman caught sight of the golden coins on Toad's table. In return for the cash, she gave Toad a cotton gown, an apron, a shawl, and a rusty black bonnet.

It was agreed that Toad would make it look like he had outsmarted the woman and stole from her. But, he did not want her to get into trouble because of him. So, it was decided that he would tie her up so it appeared the washerwoman knew nothing of his plan.

After Toad dressed, the girl giggled. "You're the spitting image of her. Good luck, Toad. Be off. But remember, you are a woman quite alone in the world now."

It seemed like hours had passed before Toad made it across the last courtyard. He was jeered and laughed at by many men. As the last gate closed behind him, he took a deep breath of the fresh air. He was free!

Toad walked quickly toward the lights of town. He had no clue as to what he would do once he arrived. When he heard the huffing and puffing of engines in the distance, he knew he must go toward the train. Lucky him! The train that was there was heading, more or less, in the direction of Toad Hall!

As Toad reached in his pocket to pay for his ticket, he realized he had left his money in the cell. He looked at the ticket master. "Look here! I left my purse behind. Just give me a ticket and I'll send the money tomorrow."

The ticket master chuckled. "Step aside. Make way for paying passengers."

Toad started to worry. Surely, someone had discovered him missing by now. The hunt would soon start. He feared he'd be caught and dragged back to prison. His punishment would be doubled. He pondered his fate, unsure of what to do next. He just had to get on that train.

Full Steam Ahead

"Hello, woman!" said the engine driver awhile later. "What's the trouble? You don't look cheerful."

"Oh, sir!" cried Toad. "I am a poor, unhappy washerwoman. I've lost my money and can't pay for a ticket. I must get home somehow."

'That's too bad," said the man. "Do you have kids waiting for you at home?"

"A lot of them," said Toad. "And they'll be hungry. Maybe even playing with matches. Most likely fighting with each other."

"Well I'll tell you what I'll do," said the man. You are a washerwoman. I'm an engine driver. There's no denying that it's very dirty work. If you wash a few shirts for me when you get home, I'll give you a ride on my engine. It's against the rules to give anyone a free ride, but I think it will be okay. We will both get something we want."

Toad couldn't believe his luck. He scrambled up the steps into the car. Of course he had never washed a shirt in his life and he wasn't about to begin.

When I get home to Toad Hall, he thought, *I'll send the engine driver money to pay for his own washing. That should be fair.*

A minute later, the train moved out of the station. As the speed increased, Toad could see fields, trees, hedges, cows, and horses fly by him. He felt happy knowing that every minute brought him closer to returning to Toad Hall. He longed for his soft bed and fancy food. He longed to see his friends.

They had covered many miles when Toad noticed the engine driver with a puzzled look on his face. He was leaning over the side of the engine and had his hand cupped to his ear. Was he trying to listen to something? He turned to Toad. "It's very strange. We're the last train running tonight. Yet, I swear I hear another train following us."

Toad slumped over. He was too afraid to think what all this could mean. By this time, the moon was shining brightly. The engine driver stood on the coal and could now see behind the train for a great distance.

"I can see it clearly now," he said. "It is an engine on our rails. It's coming toward us at a great pace. It looks as if they are chasing us."

Toad didn't say a word. He was too afraid.

"They are coming at us fast!" cried the man. "And the engine is packed with odd people. Many of them are policemen and what look like detectives. They are all shouting the same thing at us: 'Stop, stop, stop!'"

Toad fell onto the coal and clasped his paws. This was too much! "Help me! Save me! I will confess everything. I am not the simple washerwoman you think I am. I have no children waiting for me. No mouths to feed. I am Toad. The well-known and popular Mr. Toad. I have just escaped jail by being clever. If those men recapture me, I'll be put in chains. I'll have only bread and water for the rest of my days. I will once again become poor, unhappy, innocent Toad."

The engine driver looked down upon him sternly. "Now tell the truth. What were you put in prison for?"

"It was nothing awful." Toad's cheeks reddened. "I borrowed a motorcar while the owners were at lunch. I didn't mean to steal it. Honest."

The engine driver pursed his lips. "I fear that you have been a wicked Toad. But you are obviously in trouble and I will not desert you. The sight of an animal in tears makes me sad, so cheer up, Toad. I'll do my best to save you. We may outrun them yet!"

The two of them worked together and piled on more coals. The engine roared. Sparks flew and the engine leaped and swung. Still, the train behind them gained quickly on them.

The engine driver wiped his brow. "I'm sorry, Toad. It's no good. They have a better engine. There is just one thing we could do. Up ahead is a tunnel. On the other side, a thick wood follows.

"While running through the tunnel, I will go as fast as I can. Once through it, I will shut the steam off and put on the brakes. When it slows enough so it's safe, you must jump off and hide in the wood. Then I will go full speed ahead again. We will have tricked them all. They will be chasing me and only me!"

They piled on more coal as the train shot into the tunnel. The engine roared and rattled until they shot out the other end into fresh air and moonlight. Toad looked at the wood on both sides. He stepped down and when the train had slowed to a walking pace, he heard the engine driver shout, "Jump!"

Toad jumped and rolled down a small hill. He picked himself up and scrambled into the dark wood and hid. Peeping out, he saw the train pick up speed and disappear. Then, a minute later, the other train burst through the tunnel. The men were looking ahead and still screaming, "Stop, stop, stop!"

Once they passed, Toad laughed for the first time since he was thrown into prison. Soon, his laughing turned toward fear. All alone in this dark wood, he had no food or water. No money.

He walked a bit as he listened to the sounds of the Wild Wood. Sounds much too scary for him to face alone. At last, cold and hungry and tired, Toad sought shelter in the hollow of a tree. He slept soundly until morning.

CHAPTER 11

The Further Adventures of Toad

When Toad awoke the next morning, he sat up and rubbed his eyes. He had been dreaming he was at home in a warm bed. One look around, and he knew it was just a dream. He was cold and shivery. But then he remembered something important. He was free. *Free!* The word alone was worth fifty blankets.

Toad warmed up at the thought of the jolly world that awaited him. He combed the dry leaves out of his hair and marched forth into the warm sun. He was cold but confident, hungry but hopeful.

He had the world to himself this fine

morning. The dewy woodland was still. Toad longed for someone to talk to. Someone who could tell him which direction to go. He decided to follow the water's edge, figuring it led somewhere.

Round a bend came a plodding horse. Toad stepped aside to let the horse pass. It was then that he saw it was attached to a barge. Its sole occupant was a large woman wearing a sunbonnet. She sailed the barge right next to him.

"Good morning, ma'am," she remarked to Toad.

Toad responded, "Indeed, it is a good morning if you aren't in trouble like I am. I need to get to my married daughter at once. I don't know what's wrong with her but I'm fearing the worst. I'm in the washing business, you know. I left my younger children to tend to my married daughter. I've lost my way and lost all my money."

"Where does your married daughter live?" asked the large woman.

Toad spoke loudly. "Near the river. Not far from a fine house called Toad Hall. Perhaps you've heard of it?"

"Toad Hall? Why I'm going that way myself! This canal joins the river miles farther on. It brings you a little above Toad Hall but then it's just a short walk. Come along with me and I'll get you there."

The woman steered the barge close to the bank. Toad stepped on board and sat down with great satisfaction. *Toad's luck again!* he thought. *I always come out on top.*

"So, you're in the washing business?" asked the woman as they glided along.

"I'm the best there is," said Toad. "All the finest people send their clothes to me. Washing, ironing, making fine shirts. It all happens under my own eye."

"Surely you don't do all that work yourself?" asked the woman.

"I have workers, but I'm the best there is. I'm happy when I've got both arms in the washtub."

"What luck," said the woman. "I think good fortune has come to both of us."

Toad wasn't sure what she meant. He tried to change the subject, fearing what she would say next.

"There's a heap of clothes in the cabin," said the woman. "While I steer, you wash. I want to make you happy, after all."

"Why don't you let me steer?" asked Toad. He started to panic. He didn't know the first thing about washing clothes!

The woman laughed. "And deny you the joy of washing? Never."

Toad had no choice. He grabbed soap, fetched the tub, and selected a few items of clothing. He spent the next thirty minutes slapping, twisting, and punching the clothes.

Soon, his back ached. His webs were getting crinkly. He grew angrier and angrier.

A burst of laughter from behind made him stop washing. "I've been watching you the whole time," said the woman. "You are *not* a washerwoman. You've never washed a thing in your life."

Toad was angry and lost control of his temper. "I would have you know that I am Toad. I am a well-known, respected, and distinguished Toad. I will *not* be laughed at by you."

The barge woman did not like being tricked. "You are a horrid little Toad." With a flip of her arms, Toad was overboard in the cold water. *Splash!*

Toad was miffed! He swam to the shore and vowed revenge. Once ashore, he spied her horse up ahead. He jumped on its back, undid the ropes, and galloped into the countryside. Looking back, he saw the barge woman shouting, "Stop, stop, stop!" Toad laughed and rode the horse faster. That will teach her!

He had traveled some miles when his horse stopped to graze on the grass. Toad noticed a man sitting by a fire nearby. Toad could smell something wonderful cooking on his fire.

"Hello, friend," said Toad. "I'm a hungry washerwoman."

"I'll trade you some food for that horse of yours," said the man. He was a gypsy and moved quickly from place to place.

Toad was completely taken aback. He did not know that gypsies were fond of horse dealing. It had not occurred to him to sell the horse for money. But Toad wanted more than money. He wanted food and money.

"Give up my fine horse?" he said. "Out of the question. Unless you offer me lots of money *and* a morning bite to eat."

"I'll give you four shillings," said the gypsy.

"Four? Not enough!"

"I'll make it five," said the gypsy. "No more."

Toad was awfully hungry. He looked around. Were his enemies near? Five shillings would help him get home. But he wanted more.

"Look here, gypsy," Toad said. "I'll take six shillings and a meal. In return, you shall get my spirited horse with his harness thrown in for free."

The two struck a deal. Toad ate hungrily and thought this was the finest breakfast he had ever had.

The gypsy knew the riverside well and told Toad which way to go. Toad immediately set forth on his travels again in the best possible spirit.

As he marched along, he thought how luck was always on his side. *What a clever Toad I am. My enemies shut me up in prison. I escaped. They pursued me by train. I snapped my fingers at them and disappeared. I am thrown into a canal and I swim ashore and seize the barge woman's horse. I sell the horse for lots of money and a breakfast. I am the handsome, clever Toad. The popular, successful Toad.*

He sang a song about the Great Important Toad. He sang as he walked. He walked as he sang. His pride got more inflated by the minute. But his pride was shortly going to take a severe fall.

CHAPTER 12

A Familiar Face

As Toad walked on, he saw a dot in the distance. The dot turned into a blob. Then the blob turned into something that made Toad's heart thump. It was a motorcar coming down the road!

Maybe with luck I'll end up driving back to Toad Hall! he thought.

Toad stepped out in the middle of the street to hail the motorcar. As it approached, Toad's heart sank. For the approaching motorcar was the exact one that he had stolen at the pub that fateful day! And the people in it were the same people who he had stolen it from!

Toad crumpled down to the ground. *It's all over now*, he thought. *Chains and policeman again. Prison again! Dry bread and water again. What a fool I've been! Here I am thinking I've been so clever and now this! I am a sorry Toad. An ill-fated animal. A stupid, stupid, dim-witted Toad.*

The motorcar stopped. Two men got out. They walked over to the crumpled heap in the middle of the street.

"Oh, dear," said one man. "You poor washerwoman. You've fainted in the middle of the road." He looked at the driver. "Perhaps she was overcome by heat. Let's lift her into the car and take her to the nearest village. Surely she has many friends who can take care of her there."

They gently lifted Toad into the motorcar and went on their way. When Toad heard them speaking so kindly, he knew they didn't recognize him. His courage rose. His mood improved a great deal. Cautiously, he opened one eye and looked around. Then, he opened the other.

"Look," said the driver. "She is feeling better already, I think. Don't try to talk. Keep still and quiet."

"Thank you," said Toad in a feeble voice. He sat up straight. "I am feeling a great deal better. Maybe if I sit up front and get some fresh air, I'll feel even stronger."

"What a sensible woman," said the gentleman. "Of course! Of course you shall sit up here." They carefully helped Toad to the seat next to the driver. They continued once more.

Toad was almost himself again by now. He looked about and tried to beat down the yearning to drive once again. *It's fate*, he thought. *Why struggle? Why fight it?*

"Please, sir," he said. "I wish to drive. I've been watching you carefully. I'd like to tell my friends that I have driven a motorcar. I promise to be careful. Very careful."

The driver laughed. The other man thought for a moment before answering. "I like your spirit. I think we should let you have a try. What harm can it do?"

The driver made room for Toad.

Toad eagerly scrambled into the seat, took the steering wheel, and set the car in motion. At first, he drove slowly and carefully and pretended to listen to the directions that were being offered. Then Toad picked up speed. He went faster and faster and faster and faster.

The driver shouted out, "Be careful, washerwoman! Slow down. You are going too fast!"

This annoyed Toad and he began to drive even faster.

The driver tried to interfere, but Toad pinned him down with one elbow and drove at an even greater speed.

"Washerwoman, indeed," he shouted recklessly. "I am Toad. The motorcar snatcher, the prison-breaker. The clever Toad who always escapes. Sit still and you shall know what driving really is. For you are in the hands of the

famous, the skillful, the entirely fearless Toad of the grand Toad Hall."

With a cry of horror, the gentlemen flung themselves on Toad. "Seize this wicked animal who stole our motorcar!" they cried. "Bind him. Chain him. Drag him to the nearest police station. Down with the dangerous Toad!"

With all that ruckus, Toad turned the wheel and sent the car crashing through a low hedge that ran along the roadside. Toad found himself flying through the air. He felt like a Toad Bird as he landed on his back with a thump.

Sitting up, he could see the motorcar in the pond nearly submerged. The gentleman and the driver were floundering in the water and screaming at Toad.

Toad didn't wait to hear what they had to say. He picked himself up and started running as fast as he could. He scrambled through hedges, jumped ditches, and pounded across every field until he was breathless.

When he recovered his breath, he began to giggle. Immediately, he forgot his troubles. *Toad again. Comes out on top. Who was it that got them to give him a lift? Who managed to get in the front seat for the sake of fresh air? Who persuaded them to let me drive? Who landed them all in a pond but escaped? Why Toad of course! Clever, great Toad!*

Suddenly, he heard a scuffle behind him. It was two policemen chasing him! He picked himself up and ran as fast as his short legs could take him. Not looking where he was going, he soon landed in water. Deep water. The river!

"Oh my!" he gasped and he started to sink. *If I ever steal a motorcar again! If I ever think so highly of myself again!* Then down under the water he went. He caught hold of the bank and pulled himself up out of the water just in time.

The policemen were nowhere in sight. Toad sat a minute to catch his breath. To the left, he noticed a dark hole. When he looked in, he saw two eyes staring back at him. Two small eyes. The face was brown and small with whiskers.

Toad looked closer.

My goodness! he thought. *It couldn't be! It is!* It was Rat!

CHAPTER
13

Punishment

Rat put out his paw and gripped Toad firmly by the scruff of the neck. He hoisted him over the hole until at last he was safe in the hall. Toad was some sight! He was caked with mud and straw. But his spirits were high to be back in the house of an old friend.

"Oh, Ratty! I've been through such times since I saw you last. Such sufferings! I've been to prison. Escaped. Thrown into a canal but swam to safety. Stole a horse and sold him for a large amount of money. I am a smart Toad. A very smart Toad indeed. I can't wait to tell you every detail of my heroics! A lesser Toad would not have made it!"

"Toad," said Rat. He did not smile. "Go upstairs and take off your ridiculous clothes. Clean yourself up and try to come down looking like a gentleman. I have never set eyes on something so shabby in all my life."

At first, Toad was angry at the way Rat spoke to him. But then he caught sight of himself in the mirror. Rat was right! He did look shabby! It was time to spiffy up. By the time he returned, lunch was on the table. Toad was simply famished!

While they ate, Toad told Rat all about his adventures and kept repeating how clever he was. The more Toad bragged about his clever ways, the angrier Rat became.

When at last Toad was finished telling his stories, Rat said, "Toad, you've made a fool of yourself. Don't you see? You've been handcuffed, imprisoned, starved, chased, terrified, insulted, laughed at, and thrown into a canal by a woman! Where's the amusement in that? Where is the fun? And all because you had to go and steal a motorcar!

"Steal! You've never had anything but trouble from motorcars from the moment you set your eyes on one. Why steal them? You could afford many! When will you do right by your friends? How do you think we feel when we hear the animals whispering saying we are friends with you? A criminal!"

Toad suddenly felt foolish. He lowered his eyes. "Yes, Ratty. I have been a senseless Toad. I am conceited. I have too much pride. But now I will be a good Toad. As for motorcars, I'm not that keen on them since I ended up in this river of yours.

"Now, I will be a gentleman and stroll down to Toad Hall. I'll get into clothes of my own. Adventures? I've had enough. I shall lead a quiet life. A respectful life. I'll improve my property and garden a bit. No more tinkering with motorcars. I shall leave at once for Toad Hall."

Rat couldn't believe his ears. "Stroll down to Toad Hall? Are you serious? What are you talking about?" Rat chewed on his lip. "Do you mean to say you haven't heard?"

"Heard what?" asked Toad. "Go on, Ratty. Don't spare me any details. I can take it."

Rat took a deep breath. "You haven't heard a word about the Weasels and the Stoats? Not a word?"

"What? The Wild Wooders?" asked Toad. He trembled. "Not a word. What have they been doing?"

"They've taken over Toad Hall!" said Rat. "When you got into trouble over the motorcar . . ."

Rat didn't know how exactly to break it to Toad. He was unsure of what to say. "Well, it was the talk of the town, Toad. Animals take sides, you know. The riverbankers stood up for you. They said you hadn't been treated fairly and would return one day. But not so with the Wild Wood animals. They said they had heard things. Bad things. They told everyone that you deserved your punishment. They said you'd never show your face in these parts again."

Toad nodded. He wasn't sure what to say.

"Mole and Badger stuck it out through thick and thin. They knew you'd come back someday. So they arranged to move their things into Toad Hall. They wanted to sleep there and have it ready for when you returned. They didn't know just how terrible those Wild Wood animals could be. And it was terrible. So terribly terrible."

Toad's heart sank.

Rat continued on, "Now I come to the most tragic part of my story. One dark night, a band of Weasels, armed with weapons, crept silently into the carriage drive to the front entrance. At the same time, Ferrets advanced through the kitchen garden and took over the back offices. Then the Stoats overtook the conservatory and the billiards room.

"Mole and Badger fought the best they could. But they were unarmed and taken by surprise. What can two animals do against hundreds? Nothing. They retreated and the Wild Wooders have been living in Toad Hall ever since!"

Toad stood. "Oh, they have? I'll see about that!" Toad seized a stick.

"It's no good, Toad. You'll get yourself into more trouble. Stay here."

Toad didn't listen. There was no holding him back. He marched rapidly down the road, stick over his shoulder, fuming and muttering to himself, "Nothing can stop me now. Nothing can stop me from entering Toad Hall! The finest house in these parts."

But as soon as Toad approached the front gate, something did stop him. A yellow ferret popped up from the hedge and pointed a gun right at Toad.

A Secret Passage

"Who comes there?" asked Ferret.

"What do you mean talking to me like that?" said Toad angrily. "Come out here at once or I'll . . ."

Ferret never said a word. He brought his gun up to his shoulder and fired. *Bang!* A bullet whistled right over Toad's head.

Startled, Toad scampered down the road as fast as he could. As he ran away, he heard Ferret laughing at him.

"I told you," said Rat when Toad told him what had happened. "What did you expect? They are all armed. You must simply wait. It is too dangerous."

But Toad couldn't wait. He jumped into a boat and rowed to where Toad Hall met the river. As he approached, he rested his oars. All seemed peaceful and still. He stared for a moment at the entrance of Toad Hall. It would be his again. He was determined.

As he started to row under the bridge, *crash!* A great stone dropped from above smashing the bottom of the boat. It filled and sank the boat and Toad found himself struggling in the deep water.

Looking up, he saw two Stoats peering over the bridge. "Next time, it will be your head, Toad."

The indignant Toad swam to shore while the animals laughed at him. Again.

"What did I tell you?" said Rat when Toad explained his wet clothes. "Now look what you've done! You've destroyed my boat and ruined the nice clothes I lent you. I wonder how you manage to keep any friends at all, Toad."

Toad knew he had been acting foolish again. He admitted such and apologized to Rat. "Ratty, I have been headstrong and have done as I pleased. I will now be humble and will take no further action without your support."

"If you are telling the truth," said Rat, "then my advice to you is to sit and have supper. It's late. You must wait to hear the latest news from Mole and Badger."

Toad nodded. "What's become of my friends?"

Rat explained how they had been camping in the open in all sorts of weather watching over Toad's house. They provided a constant eye over the Weasels and the Stoats.

"Toad, you'll be sorry that you didn't value them more!" said Rat.

Toad sobbed. He did value their friendship and couldn't wait to tell them. He didn't have to wait long. After dinner, Mole and Badger arrived.

"Welcome home, Toad," said Badger. "I only wish you had a home to return to."

"Hooray for Toad," said Mole. "Fancy to have you back again." He began to dance around him. "We never thought you would have turned up so soon. You must have escaped you clever, ingenious, intelligent Toad!"

Before Rat could interrupt, Toad was back to his old ways. "Clever? Why if you consider breaking out of the strongest prison in England, escaping on a railroad train, and disguising myself as a washerwoman clever, then I suppose I am! Yes, I am the most clever Toad!"

Toad pulled out a pile of silver from his pocket. "Mole, guess how I got these coins? Horse dealing!"

Rat was annoyed. "Mole, don't egg him on. Instead, why not tell us about the conditions at Toad Hall? What is the latest news?"

Mole turned serious. "It's quite grave. Every animal is armed with weapons. It's a difficult situation."

The whole conversation angered Toad. "That is *my* house. I'm going to go there and . . ."

Badger stood and shouted. "Toad! You are a fool! Won't you ever learn? You are a bad, troublesome animal. What do you think your father, my old friend, would say if he were here tonight? He would not be happy with all of your foolishness."

Toad sat on the sofa and started to shake. He sobbed and proclaimed he was indeed truly sorry for acting so foolish.

Badger softened his voice. "You must truly be sorry, Toad. Let's start again. Let's come up with a plan and not be hasty. There is another way to get back your home that doesn't involve taking it by storm. Lean in. For I shall tell you a great secret."

Toad dried his eyes. He loved secrets, perhaps because he could never keep one.

Badger continued. "There is an underground passage. It leads from the River Bank to the middle of Toad Hall."

"Nonsense," said Toad. "I would have known about it."

"My dear friend," said Badger, "your father was a friend of mine. He told me things he wouldn't dare tell you. He didn't make the passage, but he discovered it. He repaired and cleaned it out. He asked me not to tell you because he knew you couldn't keep a secret. He explained that I could tell you only if you fell into a fix. And dear Toad, you are in a fix."

At first, Toad felt sulky but brightened up almost at once. "My tongue does get wagging, I suppose," Toad admitted. "Go on, Badger. How will this passage help us?"

Badger explained that Otter had disguised himself and went to Toad Hall looking for work. "He discovered there's going to be a huge party tomorrow evening. It's Chief Weasel's birthday. All the Weasels will be gathered in the dining hall. They'll be eating, drinking, and laughing. They won't have their guns. No swords. No sticks.

"The Weasels will think the Stoats will guard the outside faithfully. But you see, we will take the passage straight to the butler's pantry. It's next to the dining hall! We'll surprise them all."

With plans in place, the animals went to bed. They knew they had to be well rested to face the battle ahead.

The Return of Toad Hall

The next morning, Mole rushed into the kitchen. "I came up with a clever plan. I borrowed your washerwoman costume, Toad. I went off to Toad Hall and posed as a washerwoman looking for work.

"They laughed at me and told me to run away. I told them that it wasn't I who would be running away very soon. It was them!"

"How could you tell our plan?" said Rat.

Badger laid down his newspaper.

Mole smiled and continued, "I could see their ears prick up. Then someone said I didn't know what I was talking about.

"'Oh, I don't, do I?' said I. Then I said, 'My daughter works for Mr. Badger. And she said a hundred bloodthirsty badgers are attacking Toad Hall this very night. Six boatloads of rats, too. Everyone will come by river and meet in the garden.' Then I ran away. Of course I hid to see what they said. They were nervous and flustered. They agreed to add more protection to the garden area."

Toad frowned. "Why tell them our plans, Mole? You've spoiled everything."

Badger laughed. "Mole, how clever you are. Good job!"

Toad became jealous. He had no idea what clever thing Mole had done. But before he could lose his temper, Rat announced that lunch was waiting. And Toad simply would never miss a meal.

When it became dark, Rat summoned each one. He gave them each a belt with a sword, a pair of pistols, and a flask of water. Badger took one lantern and said, "Follow me." Mole, Rat, and Toad followed.

Badger led them along the river for some

way and suddenly swung over the ledge into a hole in the bank. Mole and Rat followed without incident. Toad, of course, slipped and fell into the water. All the splashing was sure to attract attention if Badger hadn't pulled him inside the hole so quickly.

At last, they were in the secret passage. The passage was cold, dark, damp, and narrow. Toad dreaded the thought of what was ahead of them. He lagged behind the others a bit in the darkness. They shuffled along with their ears pricked and their paws on their pistols.

At last, Badger said, "We're under Toad Hall." Voices could be heard up above.

The passage now sloped upward. The noise became louder. Stamping of feet on the floor could be heard. The clanging of glasses and fists pounding on tables rang out. What a time they seemed to be having up above. The four hurried along until they found themselves standing under the trapdoor.

It was so noisy that they didn't worry of

anyone hearing them enter the room. As they opened the door, they saw such a sight. Animals were cheering at a speech given by Chief Weasel. He was talking about Mr. Toad. The entire place broke into laughter.

"Let me at him," shrieked Toad.

Badger grabbed his stick. "The hour has come! Follow me!" With that, the heroes burst forth. The terrified Weasels hid under tables. The Ferrets rushed for the fireplace. Many a table and chairs were overturned. China crashed to the floor. Glasses smashed to the ground.

Toad headed straight for Chief Weasel. Although they were only four, to the Weasels in the hall, they looked like an army. All the animals fled screaming and screeching while seeking refuge and escape.

Mole busied himself handcuffing the animals while Badger rested. "Mole," said Badger, "go see what the Stoats are doing. Thanks to you, I don't think we'll be having much trouble from them tonight."

Mole vanished through a broken window and came back with an armful of rifles. "It's over," he reported. "As soon as the Stoats heard the shrieks, they threw down their weapons and fled. The others stood guard until the Weasels came running out. Many thought the Weasels were traitors. A great fight ensued and many rolled right into the river."

Badger smiled. "Well done, Mole. Now before we enjoy this feast, take these animals upstairs. Have them clean each room and make up the beds. Have them put clean clothes and soap in each room. Then, escort them out. We won't ever see them again. When they are gone, come back and enjoy a fine meal with us."

Mole did what he was told. At dinner, Toad spoke. "Thank you, Mole, for all your cleverness and what you did for me. You have all helped give me back my home."

The next morning, Toad came downstairs later than everyone else. Through the window of his breakfast room, he could see Mole and Rat sitting in the wicker chairs roaring with laughter. No doubt, they were sharing stories of bravery from the evening before.

Toad joined Badger for breakfast. "I'm sorry, Toad. But I'm afraid you have work to do. You ought to have a banquet at once to celebrate this affair. It's expected. In fact, it's the rule."

Toad agreed. "That's a very good idea."

Badger put down his toast. "I'm afraid you don't have time to eat. You must write out all the invitations at once."

"What?" cried Toad. "Waste all this time writing invitations on a jolly morning like this? Certainly not!" Then Toad's cheeks blushed. "Why, Mr. Badger. Of course! It is my pleasure. I am indeed indebted to all of you."

Badger looked at Toad suspiciously. Was he a changed Toad, or was he being a clever Toad once more?

Toad hurried to the writing table. A fine idea had come to him while he talked to Badger. He would write the invitations. He would hint at his adventures and his cleverness. And he would include a program of entertainment on the front. It looked like this:

Speech: By Toad
(There will be other speeches
by Toad during the evening)
Address: By Toad
Synopsis: Our Prison System ❧ The
Waterways of England ❧ Horse Dealing and
How to Deal ❧ Back to Land ❧ A Typical
English Squire
Song: By Toad: Composed by Toad

This pleased him. When the others saw how happy and pleased with himself Toad was, they started to wonder what he was up to.

CHAPTER 16

A Changed Toad

"Look here," said Rat. "There will not be any speeches at this banquet. You must understand clearly once and for all that there will be no bragging. Not through speeches, songs, or lectures. We're not arguing with you. We're telling you, Toad. How did you ever think those invitations would escape us? Lucky for us, we saw them before they were delivered. I repeat, Toad. No bragging of any kind."

Toad saw he was trapped. They knew him. They got ahead of him. His plans were ruined.

"May I sing just one little song?" he pleaded.

"No, not one little song," replied Rat firmly. Though he hated to see Toad sad, he knew he must be firm. "It's no good, Toady. All your songs are boastful. You know you must turn over a new leaf sooner or later. This seems like a splendid time to begin."

Toad remained silent. At last he raised his head. "It was a small thing I asked. However, you are right. I will be a different Toad from now on." He pressed his handkerchief to his face and left the room.

Everyone felt a bit guilty.

"It had to be done," sighed Badger. "Do we want him to become a laughingstock?"

"Of course not," said Rat.

As the hour of the banquet approached, Toad retired to his bedroom and sat there thinking. His brow rested on his paw. Slowly, he smiled. He got up, locked the door, drew the curtains closed, and arranged all the chairs in his room in a semicircle.

Toad took his position in front of the chairs and bowed. He coughed twice and let himself go. He sang the song he longed to sing as he pretended his audience was before him. When he finished, he sang it all over again!

Then Toad heaved a deep sigh. A long, long, long sigh. He dipped his hairbrush in the water jug, parted his hair, and plastered the sides down. Unlocking the door, he went quietly downstairs to greet his guests.

All the animals cheered when he entered. They crowded around to congratulate him. Everyone had nice things to say about his courage, his cleverness, and his fighting qualities. But Toad only smiled faintly and murmured, "Not at all!" or "On the contrary!"

Otter, who was standing nearby, called out, "You are a hero!"

Toad shook his head. "Badger was the mastermind. Mole and Rat did most of the fighting. I merely served in the ranks and did little or nothing."

The animals were puzzled and taken back by Toad's new attitude. Toad felt, as he moved from one guest to another, that he was the object of increasing interest. It amused him.

The banquet was a great success. Badger had done a fine job ordering everything. Throughout all of it, Toad kept complimenting others. When he saw the shocked expression on a face, he took extra delight. There were even some cries of, "Toast, Toad. Song!" But Toad only shook his head gently, raised one paw in mild protest, and asked about their families.

He was indeed a changed Toad!

After the banquet, the four animals continued to lead their lives. Toad selected a handsome gold chain and locket set with pearls to give to the jailer's daughter. He included a letter, which even Badger declared as modest, grateful, and appreciative. The engine driver was properly thanked as well. Under urging from Badger, even the barge woman was given thanks and compensation for her horse.

Sometimes in the long summer evening, the friends would stroll together in the Wild Wood. It was now tamed and they were always welcomed. It was pleasing to see how all the animals greeted them. Often, the Weasels would bring their young ones to meet them. They would say, "Look, baby. There goes the great Mr. Toad, the gallant Water Rat—a terrible fighter—and the famous Mr. Mole."

When the babies were being naughty, they would quiet them by telling them that gray Badger would get them. This, of course, was not true at all. Although Badger didn't care much for society, he was rather fond of little children.